Growing Up

W9-CDC-706

IS SUSAN HERE?

by

Janice May Udry

Illustrated by Peter Edwards

One day Susan disappeared, so her mother had a tiger help her with the dishes, an elephant hang up her clothes, a monkey go marketing with her, a pig eat her lunch and other animals keep her company all during the day. But at bedtime, who do you suppose turned up?

K

Classification and Dewey Decimal: Easy (E)

About the Author:

JANICE MAY UDRY knows just what makes up the all-important, every-day world of children. Her young daughter, Leslie, loves to pretend she is all kinds of things, just like Susan of IS SUSAN HERE?

Mrs. Udry was a library assistant at Northwestern University, then a nursery school assistant. She is a Caldecott Medal winner and one of her books was a Junior Literary Guild selection. Janice May Udry grew up in Illinois and now lives in California.

About the Illustrator:

Regents Park Zoo, in London, where the best seals live, is near the Art School that PETER EDWARDS attended. He started illustrating in Sweden, where he met and married another artist. They now live in a small house in the country, and have three children and numerous animals.

IS SUSAN HERE?

IS
SUSAN
HERE
?

by JANICE UDRY   pictures by PETER EDWARDS

1965 FIRST CADMUS EDITION
THIS SPECIAL EDITION IS PUBLISHED BY ARRANGEMENT WITH
THE PUBLISHERS OF THE REGULAR EDITION
ABELARD-SCHUMAN LIMITED
BY

E. M. HALE AND COMPANY
EAU CLAIRE, WISCONSIN

p 4990

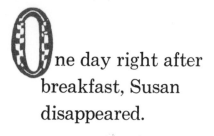

One day right after breakfast, Susan disappeared.

But while Susan's mother was clearing the table, a something came into the kitchen. "Mercy me!" said Susan's mother, "Whatever is this in my kitchen?"

"Grrr, it's a tiger," said the tiger. "Where is your little girl Susan?"

"I don't know," said Susan's mother. "But she usually helps me with the dishes."

"*I'll* help you today," said the tiger kindly.

So Susan's mother and the tiger did the dishes.

Then Susan's mother washed the clothes. Just as
she started to hang them on the clothesline,
an elephant came around the house.
It tugged at Susan's mother's apron with its trunk.
"Heavens!" said Susan's mother, dropping clothespins.
"Where did you come from, Elephant?"

The elephant picked up
the clothespins.
"Where's your little girl Susan?"
the elephant asked.
"I don't know," said
Susan's mother.
"But she usually helps me
hang up the clothes."
"*I'll* help you today,"
said the elephant kindly.

When Susan's mother
started to go to the market
a monkey met her at the door.
"Well," said Susan's
mother, "a monkey!"
The monkey began pushing
the grocery cart for her
and chattering.
"Where is your little
girl Susan?" the monkey
asked as they walked along.
"I don't know," said
Susan's mother. "But
she usually goes to market
with me."
"*I'll* go with you today,"
said the monkey. "I can
do anything Susan
can do."

p4990

Lunch time came.
While Susan's mother was stirring
some soup, a pig came in.
"Oink," said the pig, "I'm hungry."
"Would you like to eat lunch
with me?" asked Susan's mother.

"Where is your little girl Susan?"
asked the pig.
"I don't know," said Susan's mother.
"Then *I* will eat Susan's lunch
today," said the pig.
So Susan's mother had lunch
with a pig.

Then Susan's mother said to herself, "Now I'll take a little nap."
But as she was lying down on the couch, something walked up to it.
"Gracious! What is that?" asked Susan's mother.
"Grump, I'm a bear!"

"How do you do, Bear," said Susan's
mother rather sleepily.
"Grump," said the bear. "Don't you have
a little girl Susan?"

"Yes, I do," said Susan's mother, "but
she's not here. She usually takes
a nap when I do."
The bear yawned.
"*I'll* take Susan's nap today."

After her nap, Susan's mother
began to sew.
A chicken came in and sat down.
"Cluck, cluck. Is Susan here?"
the chicken asked.
"No," said Susan's mother.

"But she usually helps me
with my sewing."
"Chickens are very good at
pulling out stitches,"
said the chicken.
And the chicken pulled out
the old hems on Susan's
dresses so that her mother
could put in new ones.

After that
Susan's mother wrote a letter.
As she was starting out to mail it,
a bird flew up to the door.
"My, what a large bird," said
Susan's mother.

"Twill-o, Twill-o," sang the bird.
"Is Susan here yet?"

"No," said Susan's mother. "And she
always mails my letters for me."
"*I'll* do it today," said the bird sweetly.

Susan's father came home. When
dinner was ready, he and Susan's
mother sat down to eat. Before
they had taken one bite, a
rabbit joined them.

"My word," said Susan's father.
"A rabbit!"

"Yes," said Susan's mother,
"this house is full of animals."

"Is your little girl Susan coming
to dinner?" asked the rabbit.

"No, I guess not," said
Susan's mother.

"Then *I'll* eat Susan's dinner,"
said the rabbit,
picking up a fork. "Pass the
carrots please."

"For a rabbit," said Susan's father,
"you certainly do eat a lot."

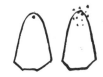

After dinner Susan's mother
and father sat down in their
big comfortable chairs.
It was very quiet.
"I miss Susan," sighed
Susan's mother.
"I miss Susan, too," said
Susan's father.
"It was nice to be helped
today by a tiger, an elephant,
a monkey, a pig, a bear,
a chicken and a bird, and
to have dinner with a rabbit,"
said Susan's mother.
"But I'd rather have dear Susan."

"Do you suppose she'll ever come back?" asked Susan's father.
"Who knows," sighed Susan's mother. "And I have no one to put to bed tonight. I think I'll just go sit awhile in Susan's room even though she is not there."

So Susan's mother went into Susan's room and sat down in the rocking chair. She even sang the song Susan liked best to hear at night.

Then, very softly, someone came in.
"I'm back," said Susan.

　　　　　　And she was.